# The S

## An Extreme Horror Story

By Alana K. Drex & A.W. Mason

Arrow Pig Press, Tampa, FL

Chap Book first edition

ISBN: 9798837185908

*Cover Design and Illustrations by TrubornDesign*

Published by Arrow Pig Press

## The Scampering

*Bitterness becomes an entity of its own making. And when it's uncontainable, it spreads…*

*-Unknown*

Melinda saw the tiny gray tuft streaking across the road, held her breath and thought, *he's going to make it.* She picked up speed, clamping down on the accelerator. The squirrel turned, startled by the car's roaring drone, and then out of sheer panic it froze. The creature sped back the way it had come, ending up under the left front wheel of the car. She was sure he'd been hit as he didn't pop out across the other lane into the fortress of tall grass. A mirror check showed the thing was laid out on its back, a hind leg twitching. An evil chortle escaped her lips.

Melinda rounded the block to go back and take another look at the scene, glancing in her side mirror as she did. In the reflection she saw the deep scar across her forehead, a gash she'd have to live with the rest of her life. Her husband though, he wasn't so lucky. Melinda thought back to the day almost a year and a half ago when two gray squirrels darted across the road as her husband, Michael, drove them to their favorite restaurant for date night. The roads were dry and the light of the day still lingered but he nevertheless lost control of the vehicle to avoid hitting those two mischievous little creatures.

The sedan careened into an old oak, its massive trunk stopping the car like a child's toy. However, unlike a child's toy, the impact shattered the windshield, and a flying piece of glass akin to shrapnel raked across Melinda's forehead as her body lunged against her seatbelt from the impact. A thick branch impaled the driver's side of the windshield, entering Michael's left eye socket, piercing through to the back of his skull. The momentum of the wreck locked his seatbelt too and projected him forward, easily ripping his head from his body as the oak branch skewered his cranium like a macabre shish kabob. His neck dripped with hot, sticky blood and ran down the sinewy gore of the flaps of skin still dangling from his throat.

The traumatic memories arose like noxious fumes hissing from beneath the scrunched hood of a wrecked car; stinging and bringing tears to her eyes. The effects of those fumes long-term however were still in progress within her, toying with her brain's chemistry the more they remained. So far, Melinda was a numb and bitter shell most days. Although, this current happy accident had made her laugh for the first time in she didn't know how long. So, she decided to focus on that. And as she did, a quiver began deep in the recesses of her belly—a genuine laugh that soon turned painfully violent—as it crossed her mind she may have killed some squirrel bitch's lover. She'd call him Bob for simplicity. Tit for tat.

As Melinda circled the block, she was able to replay that whole scene in her head before happening upon the nearly dead squirrel again, smiling at the aftermath. Maybe this was even a descendant of the conniving murderers that took her husband. Two fat crows took turns pecking at him like one of those tacky desk accessories. They were comically swift at their task of tearing flesh from bone, delighted at their steaming meal. She hoped that fucker stayed alive long enough for this part. *Did the foot twitch again just now?* Her laughter turned to vicious chuckles that strained her abdominal muscles further. Cradling her stomach with one hand, she tightened her grip on the wheel with the other to ensure she didn't run Bob over a second time. It would be a pity to bring any mercy to his torturously prolonged dying moments.

Once free and clear, she glanced in the rearview mirror again, now aware of a gaggle of six children standing on the sidewalk mere yards away from the crushed critter. Some were gaping at it, but two girls stared after her instead, mouths wide open in twin O's of utter shock.

*       *       *

She pulled her nearly decade old SUV into their— her—long driveway at just before noon, deciding on a late lunch. Melinda had some fliers to type up and distribute, she hummed the old '70s song "Taking Care of Business" under her breath.

The neat two-story home with a two-car garage rested atop a gentle slope. "Perfect for sledding," Michael had said when they were still deciding on their ideal family home. He had made a lot of comments on that tour. *The fenced area in the back would be great for small kids. The bookshelves are built-ins so there won't be any risk of crushing little climbers.* They'd immediately put in an offer.

*I won't think of this*, Melinda decided abruptly, *I can wallow later, I have important action to take first.*

6

Rolling to a stop in front of the garage, she popped the gear into park and grabbed the fresh ink cartridge beside her from her morning errands. Melinda never used the garage. Its empty second space reminded her too much of Michael and the practical four door sedan he'd purchased excitedly for their future family in the same week they began seriously trying for a baby. The same sedan with the busted-out windshield and crumpled hood. Red splotches on white paint. Because white cars are cheaper than other cars of the same make and year. And Michael is…*was* nothing if not caring and thoughtful…

Melinda ran toward the door and her next task, hoping the depressing memories would rush off as she ran, to be carried away in the wind.

"I'm so glad I have the community's wellbeing to think about," she said aloud to herself as she entered her home and made her way to the computer desk, never locking the door behind her. Personal safety was not anything she had the mental space or energy inside her to worry over *these days*. No, her community work was what mattered most *these days* as a widow.

Melinda approached her desk and tapped the space bar, bringing the monitor back to its full glow, then clicked into Word. She typed feverishly, still standing there, hunched over the keyboard. The rush of words came to her quickly, and the flier was finished in a few minutes. Would have been sooner had she not felt the need to find the perfect piece of clipart to position before the text of the document. The picture showed a squirrel with evil eyes and devil horns, grasping a tiny pitchfork. The text read:

**PSA from your local Wildlife Dept:** The population of squirrel is at a detremental number and we are asking you to do your part to bring it down. Don't pity these pests. Read below for ideas to hepl to bring down the EVIL SQUIRREL population:

1. Use lethal Traps
2. Use reg traps only with rat poison inside
3. Knock all nests down and put kits in a tied plastic bag inside your trashe receptacle

Thanks for helping your community in this most desperite time!! Remember Squirrels are NOT cute, they are EVIL!!!

Melinda gave it a quick read-over a second time, squashing down any feelings of guilt about impersonating the Wildlife Department as she installed the new ink cartridge. She knew those feelings were only because she was worried about any repercussions, which she felt made her a bad wife. Why would she worry about getting some kind of slap on the wrist, when her husband was six feet under? Besides, she wasn't signing her name to this, and nobody paid much attention to whom did what these days anyway, especially not a woman in baggy clothes who made them feel uncomfortable. Michael would be proud of her taking action. *Maybe I'll do something for myself afterwards*, Melinda thought, gathering the pile of 100 fliers from the printer tray and stalking off to her car.

Now she sat in the cushy chair at Nail Time, getting a mani-pedi. Michael always preferred funky colors on her, said they went with her personality. She'd chosen a chartreuse green today for her nails. Leaning back in the chair she smiled to herself. She knew that some people, upon reading the fliers, would be too weak to bring themselves to the dire task. But then there were many who would comply, even if they didn't like the idea, just for the fact an official department told them to do so. Then, there would be some who relished the killing anyway, jumping on the opportunity like fleas on a mangy dog.

A sudden noise interrupted Melinda from her reverie. It was a loud squelching growl, like the roar erupting from a lion's drooling jaws, causing the small nail tech to flinch and look up at her from Melinda's feet. There was a startled gleam to her liquid brown eyes that gave Melinda the urge to explain the abrupt sound.

"Oh, I guess dead squirrels give me an appetite," Melinda chuckled, even though she knew that wasn't the whole story. She had missed lunch! When was the last time she had eaten a real meal? *I'll pick up something quick on the way home.* She knew just the thing…

Unfortunately, the meal she really wanted had been picked over too much, but Melinda had seen something fresher on the way to the salon. Stopping now, she grabbed a plastic grocery bag, one in a stash of many she kept in her car for such endeavors. It was still summer so, it was best to get the carcasses fresh anyway; if they baked too long in the sun, she found them to be tougher. The reaction she got from peeling dead squirrels off the road varied. She'd heard "thank you for cleaning up the roads" and "lady you could get a disease that way, best to let it be." Melinda didn't care for the approval or disapproval, in any case. All she could think of was biting into the hide of the demonic little creatures that caused more accidents a year than anyone probably realized.

How many car crashes were actually caused by these evil assholes? In the thousands, she was sure of it. Why, how easy these little buggers could cause a fatal accident and just scamper away, and none would be the wiser. The accident would go on to be blamed on the blinding sun, over-exhaustion, or even glancing at the radio display too long. But Melinda knew the truth. Oh, she knew. And she took great satisfaction in gnashing her teeth, latching on and whipping her head side to side; turning into a monster, albeit one on a mission. And she took great delight in it. Did she ever!

And lately she was having a hard time convincing herself to wait and cook the bastards before ripping into them. So, she came to a compromise. Melinda would allow herself to bite one ear off on the car ride home. Biting into the flesh connecting the ear to the skull and sliding her teeth back and forth, back and forth in a pleasing sawing motion. Melinda always made sure to savor the action and the time it took to separate ear from squirrel. She usually had it done by the time she got home, picking up the pace if it was a shorter distance, or taking her time if it was farther out. Because as soon as she got home, she needed to boil the little kitties—this made it easier to skin them. But after that was done the experimenting began. One time she'd deep fried it, another time made it into trash tacos. A friend of hers (her only friend now), had sent her a link for the trash tacos, and she had to say, with squirrel meat, *they were divine.*

After scooping the creature from the blacktop— easy to peel up, it must have flipped around the tire, breaking its little neck on the pavement—she got back in her SUV. The engine barely had time to turn over before the little nub of an ear was being worked between her gritting front teeth. She held it with her left hand while she put her car in drive and swung back out onto the road using her knees. The seven- and-a-half-minute drive didn't seem to register. One minute she was driving, the next parking back in front of the garage. The little ear was now severed, resting like communion on her tongue.

She leaned back and closed her eyes in rapture, taking a deep breath through her nose while she rubbed the tiny flap of skin between her tongue and the roof of her mouth. *Michael, all the squirrels are wishing they'd never fucked with you now, babe*, she thought with a lopsided smile, eyes still shut.

*Knock knock knock!* The heavy fist on her driver's window made her jump and almost choke on the piece of flesh. She quickly gulped it down. "What?" she asked in a feeble voice, for there was an angry-looking woman glaring in at Melinda.

"I KNOW YOU'VE SEEN MY DOG!!" the woman—her neighbor—shouted, accentuating her words with pounding fists.

Melinda raised her arms, forgetting to drop the squirrel in her left hand. She didn't even know her neighbor's name, only that she had about eight or nine or ten dogs across the highway that she let roam free. One had been killed on the road just last year. Melinda couldn't help the nasty smirk that came over her face as she thought to herself, *it was justice*. That dog could have caused a fatal accident too.

The neighbor lady's look changed from aggressive to flabbergasted as she took in the dead squirrel still swinging from her hand.

Melinda opened the door and the neighbor lady took frenzied steps backward. "This maybe isn't a good time, but this isn't the last of it. I know I saw Mackey over here a few days ago and he never came home. I've seen the traps in the back. And, you know you wouldn't talk to me the other times I came over and knocked on your door. If you got nothing to hide, why didn't you talk?"

Melinda threw the dead carcass at the woman, hitting her in the face. The woman made a deep groan from her belly and turned, stumbling across the yard, tripping over the mole hills and yelping as she did so, as if she believed the deranged Melinda would give chase with her furry weapon of choice.

Leaving the roadkill and her neighbor to fend for themselves, Melinda crept around her side yard to check her traps. If she was lucky, she'd have a fresh meal waiting for her to prepare, and if she was really lucky, the rodent would still be alive. While scouring the internet one day, that oh so great world of endless possibilities, she came across a method of cooking, much like lobster, that entailed boiling the creature alive. It was said it made the meat taste better. Melinda heard the squirrel before she saw it; the poor bastard scratched at the mechanism pinning it down, clawing for escape.

"Hello, my lovey," Melinda said, taking the trap, and her next meal, into the house.

The sun had already started to set, leaving an eerie glow to the kitchen in the scant daylight. A large pot roiled on the stove. On the counter next to it, some chopped up onions and carrots were ready to join the rodent already floating in the soon to be stew. Melinda hummed to herself as she added a dash of this and a pinch of that from her spice rack. The meal was almost ready.

The dining room table was set for two, always set for two. Michael's empty plate and chair stood as a monument to his existence within her, his flame of eternal memory ignited in every corner of Melinda's deranged, grief-stricken mind. She said grace and plunged a steak knife into the squirrel's soft belly. Juices flowed from the corners of her mouth as she chewed the tender meat. She savored each bite but left half of the meal for the morning. Squirrel burritos were on the menu for breakfast.

After dinner, Melinda retired to her bedroom upstairs and donned her night wear. It was one of Michael's old tee-shirts, big and baggy on her frame but comforting to her nonetheless. It wrapped around her like a warm hug. She grabbed a handful of the loose sleeve and breathed it in.

From the window, a gentle breeze caressed her exposed skin, giving her a pleasant sensation of gooseflesh. During the early summer, Melinda left the upstairs windows open a smidge to let in the fresh air and fragrant aroma of the lilacs growing behind her back fence. She smiled and turned off the bedroom light, letting the moon's glow guide her to her bed. The down feather pillows seemed so inviting once her head hit the fluffy mass and sleep soon overtook her.

The digital alarm clock read 4:03 a.m. when Melinda stirred from her sleep. The faint sound of tapping danced in from the open window. Groggily, she swung her feet onto the floor and walked toward the noise, rubbing the deep sleep from her eyes. She squinted through the open blinds, her eyes still adjusting to the moonlight. Nothing. The noises had ceased and nothing seemed to move. The night was still.

Satisfied, Melinda zombie-walked back to her bed and laid down again. She smiled as she settled into the soft mattress and thought of her husband as she waited to drift off once more. The curtains fluttered around the window. The breeze was back. She was content. If her eyes had been open, she would have seen the alarm clock turn to 4:05 a.m., the exact minute all hell broke loose.

The fluttering curtains began to quake as the racket of tiny click-clacking filled the room. The noise echoed off the hardwood floors. Melinda opened her eyes, startled, but all was quiet again. She got to her feet once more, walked over and shut the window. She turned around and her face was met with the razor-sharp agony of tiny, furry claws latching onto her face.

"Noooo!" Melinda cried out to the no longer empty room as the squirrel dug its tiny sharp claws into her fleshy cheeks, ripping back small scraps of skin. Warm blood poured from her wounds and covered her chin. The rodent snapped its head back and plunged its sharp teeth into her left eye. The soft organ popped like a poached egg, gelatinous ooze dripping from her socket.

The melee happened so quickly Melinda thought for a moment that she was still dreaming. There was no way she was being attacked in her own home, her own bedroom. There was no way her mortal enemies, those filthy fucking creatures, came for her.

But what made Melinda painfully aware that the attack was indeed occurring, was a sharp pain shooting up her right leg as another set of razor-like teeth sank into her Achilles tendon. The rodent ripped it out from beneath its demure fleshy protection, severing it from her body. Melinda tried to step forward but her leg would not support her weight and she went crashing through her bedroom door and into the hall. She groped for the assailant still attached to her face and tore it free—losing a three-inch strip of her cheek in the process—and threw the thing down the stairs now in front of her.

Blood leaked from her face like a faucet. The slick liquid splattered onto the wooden floor beneath her as she felt more claws, more teeth plunge into her back. Again, she tried to stand, this time using her uninjured leg. Melinda was able to get to her feet, dragging the mangled right ankle behind her. She tried to yell, to scream, but everything that came from her mouth sounded like a garbled underwater message. The front door. She knew she had to get out of the house. That was her only hope of someone seeing the assault. Slowly, she dragged herself toward the stairs.

Outside, the neighborhood rested peacefully. Perhaps a few early risers were enjoying a fresh cup of coffee, or maybe a crossword from the morning newspaper. The air was unmoving and the dawn was still waiting to spring. Inside, however, was a carnival of horrors. The upstairs hallway seemed painted in red from the blood spray patterns left by the ravenous beasts continuously attacking Melinda. She reached out for the stair rail, only six inches away, but the squirrels had other plans.

A big gray ball of speed leaped onto Melinda's back as she reached for the banister. The sudden weight of the creature attached to her shoulder blades propelled her forward. She tried to balance herself, stepping forward with her right foot but the pool of blood covering the landing caused her to slip, simultaneously snapping her ankle sideways. Headfirst she toppled down the flight of stairs, bouncing from wall to railing, looking like some sort of bloody stuntman until she came to a rest mere feet from the front door.

"Mmlffff," Melinda managed as she laid sprawled on her back. The crescent window at the top of the door created a kind of spotlight on her body. She could feel everything. She could lift her head just a few inches to see white shards of bone tearing through her ruined legs. Her jaw was broken and hung agape like she was in the process of screaming. A number of her own teeth lodged in her throat. Underneath her, several of the rodents that took the tumble down the stairs with her squirmed under her weight, trying to escape. She could feel it all and oh how she wished she had been paralyzed. How she wished she was dead.

The sound of scurrying started again, this time from the tile in the kitchen. Melinda shifted her eyes and saw dozens of gray and black masses running at her. Running for her. In a second, they enveloped her broken body, scores of teeth ripping the night shirt off her torso. The next wave of beasts ripped at her naked flesh, devouring her inches at a time. The area around her collar bone had been chewed done to the ivory. Both nipples were ripped from her breasts, two rodents fighting over the left one, pulling it back and forth until it tore free.

Melinda wanted to scream. *Why am I still alive? Why am I still conscious?* A trail of furry creatures traversed her bloodied chest, lined up and gunned for her mouth. The first to reach latched on to her lower jaw, forcing it down even farther past its broken hinge. More tendons and tissues popped as the rodent applied its weight. Like gophers, the squirrels one by one burrowed into her mouth, crawling down her throat on the way to her stomach until her belly stretched like a grotesque beach ball.

Tears streamed in silent rivulets from Melinda's eyes, mixing with the blood and sticky gore on what was left of her face. She prayed that the shock of pain would consume her and release her from this hell. Instead, the intense fire of fresh cuts stung her inner thighs as the rodents began gnawing at the tender flesh of her upper legs. The sensation of her cotton panties being shredded from her hips followed, the squirrels finally stripping her nude. Then the real pain started.

A gray arm shot out and pawed at the slit between her open legs, pulling back the folds of her flesh. It plunged head first into her hole like a bizarre reverse birth, burrowing farther into the depths of her body until its poofy tail disappeared inside of her. She felt her bladder release while more sharp claws dug into the inside of her vaginal walls. One by one, the rodents entered her, filling up her small and large intestines, shredding her insides like a blender attachment.

From above, the casual observer might see a corpse, flesh rippling from some unknown malady within it. Melinda blinked, only one eye shutting after the other's lid became chewed off from the eye incident in her bedroom. Maybe it was a God somewhere showing mercy but the ravaged woman at the bottom of her stairs expired just before the litter of squirrels burst forth from her stomach and chest. The creatures flowed from the dead body, squirming like fat, bloody maggots. And then all at once, it was over. The rodents fled and Melinda's carcass stared up at her popcorn ceiling, the light from her good eye extinguished.

\*       \*       \*

"Open up! I know you're in there!" the neighbor lady shouted as she banged on Melinda's front door.

The sun had risen and splashed the neighborhood with warm light. Birds chirped from their homes in the trees and the smell of reclaimed water flooded the block as several houses had their sprinklers going. The neighbor lady, with renewed confidence, being removed from the situation with Melinda yesterday, continued to pound on the door. She wanted answers about her missing pooch, damnit.

"If you don't open up, I'm coming in!" she warned. The brass door knob stared up at her, almost daring her to turn it, so the neighbor lady did. The door was unlocked. She pushed the door forward and was smacked in the face with a stench that could only mean death. The neighbor lady covered her nose and once her eyes adjusted to the darkness of home, she looked down and saw what was left of Melinda.

In the street behind her, a car rolled past as the neighbor lady screamed. Her hands moved from her nose to her mouth and she froze. She wanted to step back, step away from this gruesome discovery. The sides of her vison blurred and her skin became tight on her body. She was going to pass out, she knew the feeling well enough, but still she tried to will herself to step away from the horror that lay before her. Her heart raced.

Instead, the neighbor lady stepped forward and leaned over Melinda's body. A noise not unlike stirring a large pot of macaroni and cheese seemed to emanate from the dead woman's mouth. Now holding her nose again, the neighbor lady craned her neck closer to the sound, then it stopped. She paused, trying to figure out what it was, what had happened. Before she could create any logical ideas, in a streak of gray and blood, a squirrel shot forth from Melinda's mouth, affixing itself onto the neighbor lady's face. She opened her mouth to scream and the rodent used the opportunity to burrow into her esophagus. The sudden assault caused the neighbor lady to trip backwards, smacking her skull onto the hard cement. Blood pooled under her head.

The sound of scampering filled the neighborhood as        it        began        to        wake.

# Bonus Recipe for Melinda's Famous Trash Tacos

Looking to feed a crowd of hungry little critters at your next party? Try making Melinda's Famous Trash Tacos, sure to be a hit at office parties, birthday shindigs or anytime someone wants you to bring over a new and exciting dish!

Prep time: 15 mins

Cook time: 45 mins

Total time: 1 hour

Serves: 20

Ingredients:

- Canola oil
- 1 large onion, finely minced

- 5 pounds ground squirrel (or beef or turkey for those with squeamish tummies)

- 10-15 tablespoons taco seasoning

- ½ cup chipotle hot sauce, optional

- 1 tablespoon cayenne pepper, optional

- 60 corn tortillas

- 1 pound shredded Mexican blend cheese

- Shredded lettuce

- Seeded and diced tomatoes

- Hot Sauce

- In a large skillet, heat ¼ canola oil, add onion and squirrel then cook until browned. Add taco seasoning (experiment with the hot sauce and cayenne for an extra kick!)

- In a skillet, heat canola oil then lay in a tortilla to soften it. Add ¼ cup of meat mixture and a tablespoon of cheese to the middle of the tortilla. Fold tortilla in half and press flat with a spatula

• Cook both sides until slight brown and crispy

• Once finished, transfer to a baking sheet lined with paper towels to absorb any extra oil or squirrel juices

• Repeat until all tortillas are used then serve. Top with lettuce, tomato and hot sauce

# Thank You

The authors would like to thank Kristina Osborn at TrubornDesigns for creating the wonderful illustrations and cover art. Thanks also to Hamelin Bird (author of *Wayward Suns* and *Woolie*) for reading through *The Scampering* and offering his astute advice as well as Kristina Swoboda for a final read through. Also, thanks to Christopher Robertson for the help with formatting this chap book. And to you, dear reader, for purchasing our story and helping out the Animal Welfare Institute, for which the proceeds of this work will be donated.

# About the Authors

**Alana K. Drex** always knew she wanted to write messed up stories. She is most intrigued by taking something normal and seeing how messed up she can make it. Her short story *Thresher Creeping, Blood Moon Weeping* was published by Bloodrites Horror in the anthology, *Pulp Harvest*. Currently, she is busy writing short stories and illustrating them for her horror collection, date to be determined. Alana lives in Missouri with her family and Boston Terrier, Phantom. You can follow her on Instagram (@alana.k.drex).

**A.W. Mason** lives in Florida with his cat Wallace, a retired extreme parkour artist (who looks so dapper in his little helmet and knee pads). He enjoys great beer, all the nachos and constantly tries to convince himself he actually likes running.

He is a graduate of the University of South Florida with a degree in communications, whatever that is.

His first book, *A Haunt of Travels*, is a short story collection with tales of horror, terror, suspense, crime and science fiction. His Second book, *The Cleanup Crew*, will be a weird fiction novella available in 2022. You can follow him on Instagram (@holden_beerfield) and Twitter (@AWMasonAuthor).

Printed in Great Britain
by Amazon